BEATRIX POTTER ™

COLORING BOOK

FREDERICK WARNE
An Imprint of Penguin Random House LLC

FREDERICK WARNE
Penguin Young Readers Group
An Imprint of Penguin Random House LLC

First published in the United Kingdom in 2016 by Frederick Warne.
First published in the United States of America in 2017 by Frederick Warne, an imprint of
Penguin Random House LLC, 345 Hudson Street, New York, New York 10014.

Manufactured in China

ISBN 9780141377483

10 9 8 7 6 5 4 3 2 1

THIS BOOK BELONGS TO

..

THINGS TO FIND

An empty dish

An inquisitive mouse

A flickering flame

A watering can

A business mouse

A ladybug

A resting iron

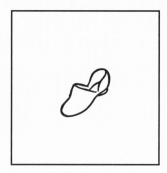

A missing shoe

A fly

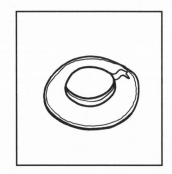

A stylish hat

A curtseying mouse

A perching robin

Peter Rabbit, Benjamin Bunny, Jemima Puddle-duck,
and so many more timeless characters await your
arrival in the enchanting world of Beatrix Potter.
Rediscover the magic of the natural world with this intricately
illustrated coloring book featuring quotes from the original tales.

Inside this book you will find delightful illustrations of
Beatrix Potter's charming characters. Add color to bring them to life
and explore the pages to find the items listed on the opposite page.

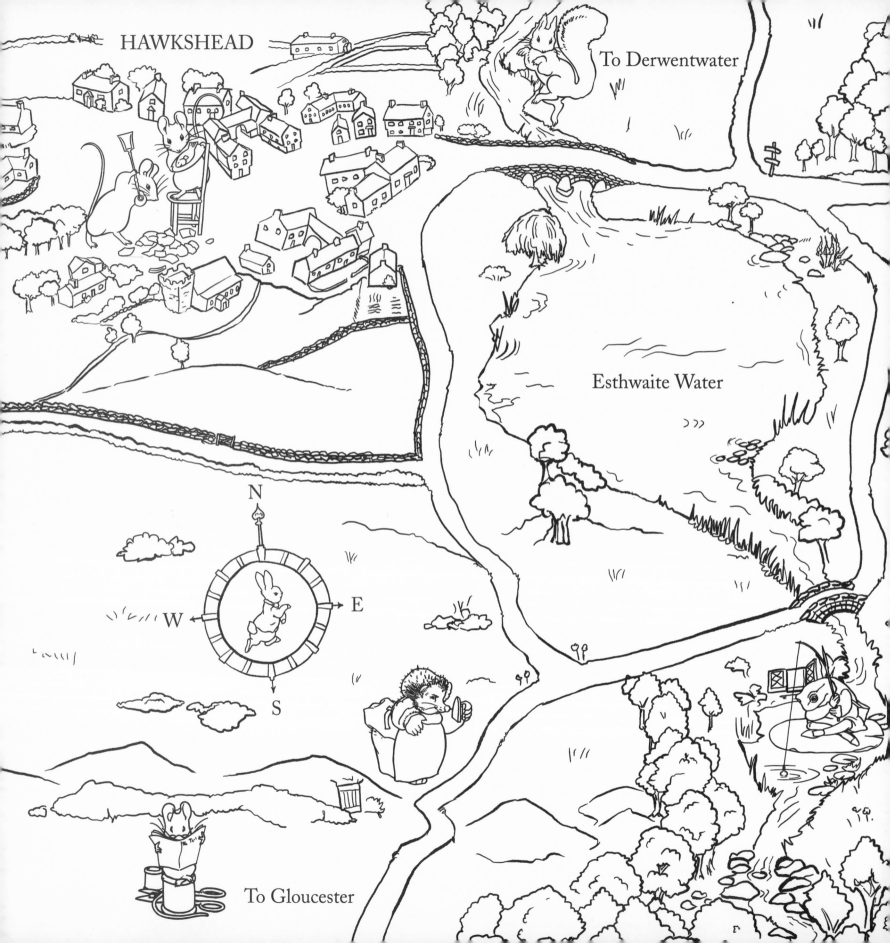

HAWKSHEAD

To Derwentwater

Esthwaite Water

N

W E

S

To Gloucester

Bull Banks

Mr. Tod's
Winter House

MAP OF
BEATRIX POTTER'S
WORLD

Ginger &
Pickles'
Shop

SAWREY

Hill Top
Farm

To Lake Windermere

Mr. Tod's
Summer House

Mr. McGregor's
Garden

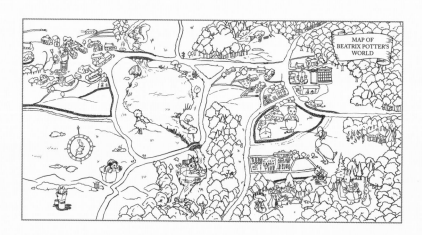

Map of Beatrix Potter's world

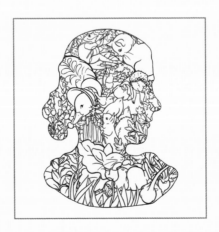

The imagination of Beatrix Potter

Peter Rabbit

In Mr. McGregor's garden

"Once upon a time there were four little Rabbits . . ."

Carnations and geraniums

Squirrel Nutkin

Sacks filled with nuts

"This is a tale about a tail . . ."

Oak leaves and acorns

The Tailor of Gloucester

"The stitches of those button-holes were so small – *so* small –
they looked as if they had been made by little mice!"

The Mayor of Gloucester's waistcoat

Jemima Puddle-duck

"Jemima thought him mighty civil and handsome."

Floating feathers

Tom Kitten

"Once upon a time there were three little kittens,
and their names were – Mittens, Tom Kitten, and Moppet."

Pansies and roses

Mr. Jeremy Fisher

"Mr. Jeremy put on a macintosh and a pair of shiny goloshes..."

Pond life

Mrs. Tiggy-winkle

"And she hung up all sorts and sizes of clothes . . ."

Hedgehogs and forget-me-nots

Two bad mice

"She found some tiny canisters upon the dresser,
labeled – Rice – Coffee – Sago . . ."

Hunca Munca and the cradle

Mrs. Tittlemouse

"When it was all beautifully neat and clean,
she gave a party to five other little mice . . ."

Butterflies, beetles, and bees

Benjamin Bunny

"The lettuces certainly were very fine..."

Onions and lettuces

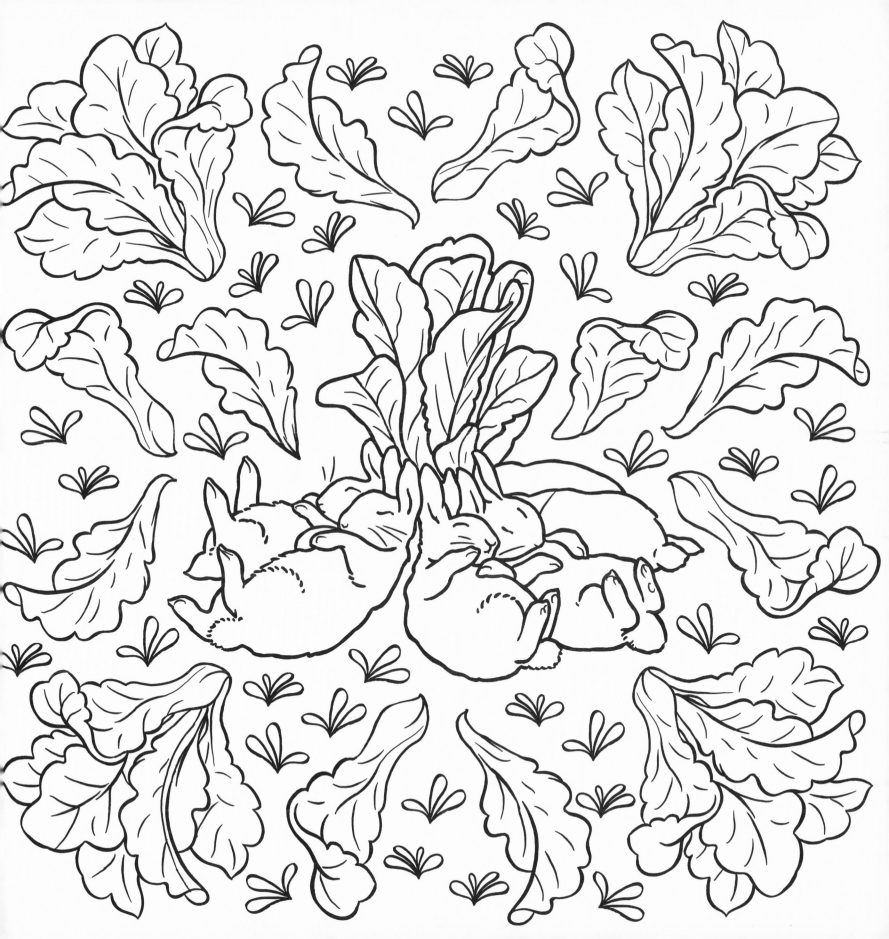

The Flopsy Bunnies

"One day – oh joy! – there were a quantity of overgrown lettuces..."

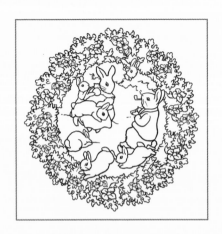

A family affair

A maze of lettuces

Ginger & Pickles' shop

"Ginger was a yellow tom-cat and Pickles was a terrier."

Strawberry shade

Timmie Willie

Miss Moppet and the Mouse

In the woods

The world of Beatrix Potter